Kalz
ion: Tracy Kaehler
ector: Keith Griffin
rector: Carol Jones

an edition published in 2006 by
low Books
or Boulevard

MN 55416

indowbooks.com

shed in Australia by
tion Pty Ltd
023
2022
2037
518 4222; Fax: (02) 9518 4333
@blake.com.au
.com.au

the United States of America.

Congress Cataloging-in-Publication Data
Lisa, 1969-
India / by Lisa Thompson ; illustrated by
son.
(Read-it! chapter books. SWAT)
mber and Jeremy enjoy many interesting and well-
s in India while on a mission for the Secret
nture Team to help find a very special creature
n a snake charmer.
8-1676-3 (hardcover)
ure and adventurers—Fiction. 2. Lost and found
—Fiction. 3. Snakes—Fiction. 4. Bombay (India)—
. India—Fiction.] I. Title. II. Series.
Inc 2005

Incred

Ind

written and illu
Lisa Thom

Editor: Ji
Page Produ
Creative D
Editorial

First Amer
Picture Wi
5115 Excel
Suite 232
Minneapoli
877-845-83
www.pictur

First pub
Blake Edu
CAN 074
Locked Ba
Glebe NSW
Ph: (02)
Email: ma
www.askbl

Printed

Library
Thompson
Incredib
Lisa Th
p. cm.
Summary
known
World
stolen
ISBN 1
[1. Ad
possess
Fiction
PZ7.T3
[E]—dc
200502

Every e
reprodu
printin

Table of Contents

TAJ MAHAL-AGRA
INDIA
SHIVA DANCING
ARABIAN SEA

S.WAT
MISSION
007
AGRA
GANGES RIVER
VARANASI
India
MUMBAI
BAY OF BENGAL
DESTINATION

CHAPTER 1

The Mission

Tick ... tick ... tick ... tick ... tick ....
Amber had been staring at the clock for the past 29 minutes and 24 seconds. The bell finally rang, and she gathered her stuff and fled the classroom. She made a beeline for the crowded bus stop.

As usual, all of the seats were taken—except one, next to Jeremy Hodgson.

"Great. Just my luck," mumbled Amber. "O.B., you have to make some room so I can sit down."

"O.B." stood for "Odd Ball," which is what everyone at school called Jeremy. Amber thought it was a name that suited him well.

"My name is Jeremy!" said Jeremy.

"Sure, whatever. Now please make some more room," said Amber.

She climbed over him and plopped herself down by the window.

"Do you know that man?" asked Jeremy, pointing out the window.

Amber turned and saw a man wearing dark glasses and a black cap, waving a piece of paper.

"I think he wants to give you that piece of paper," said Jeremy.

Amber reached out the window. She grabbed the paper just as the bus took off.

Amber and Jeremy, welcome
to SWAT. What you are about
to read is classified as
top secret.
SWAT stands for Secret
World Adventure Team. We
have a database of every
child in the world. This is how
we choose our special
secret agents.

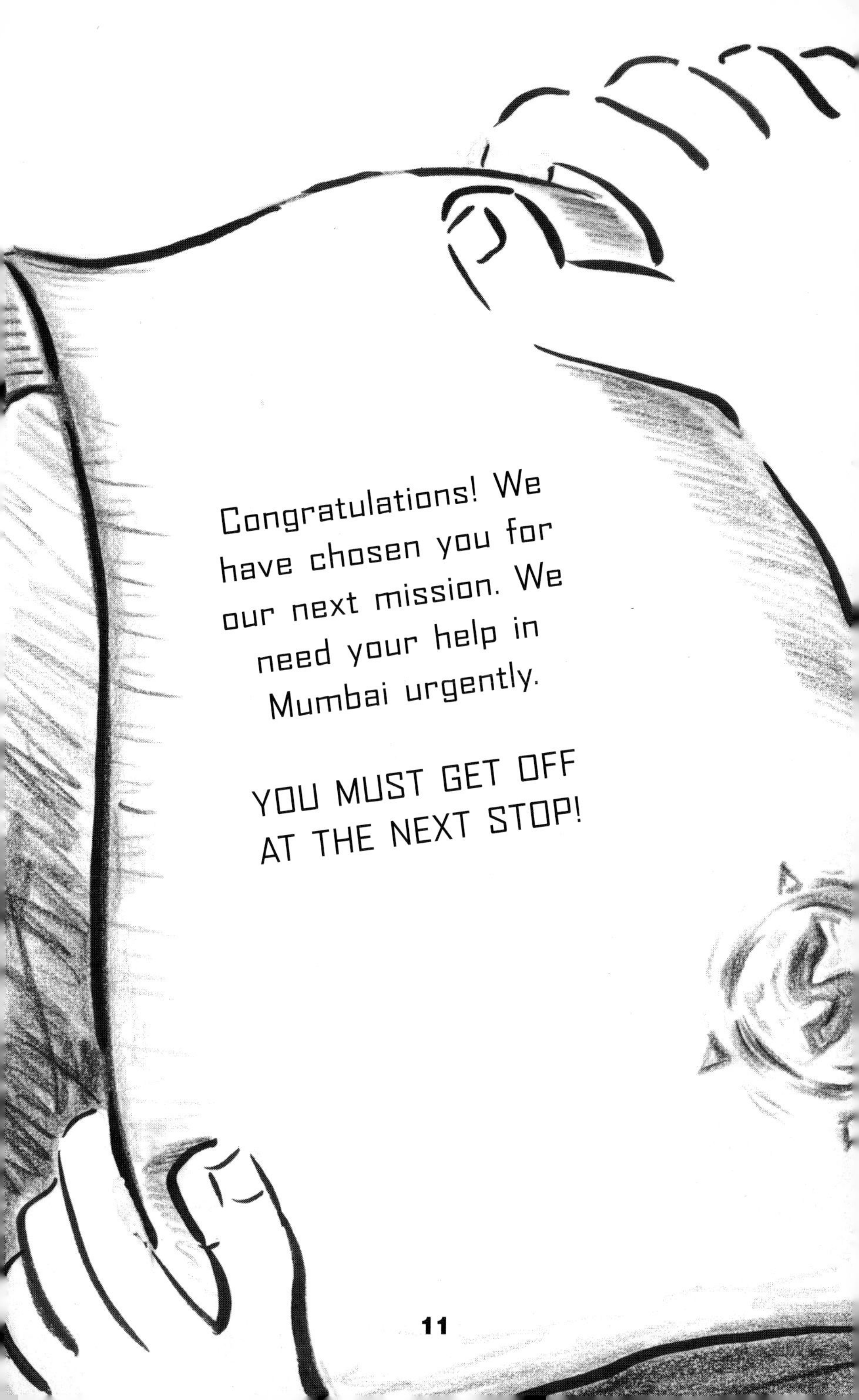
Congratulations! We have chosen you for our next mission. We need your help in Mumbai urgently.
YOU MUST GET OFF AT THE NEXT STOP!

"What do you think you're doing?" asked Amber, looking at Jeremy.

"Getting off the bus. We've got a mission to complete," answered Jeremy.

"This sounds serious," said Amber. "I really don't think this is a job for an O.B. Let me check it out, and you can continue doing whatever oddballs do."

"Look, I told you before to stop calling me that," said Jeremy, taking the paper from Amber. "My name is on that piece of paper, and I'm going."

"OK, OK! Settle down," said Amber. "Just my luck! I'm finally picked to go on a top secret mission, and I'm paired up with an O.B." Amber shook her head in disbelief.

"Hey, O.B., do you have any idea where Mumbai is?" yelled Amber, as she tried to catch up to Jeremy. He was already halfway up the street.

"India," replied Jeremy. "It used to be called Bombay, but in 1996 the Indian government renamed it Mumbai."

Amber gasped. "We're going to India?"

Jeremy finally stopped. "Here we are," he said.

"Where exactly is 'here'?" asked Amber.

The two of them stood outside a building called the Mata Hari Yoga Center. Jeremy checked the directions on the note just to make sure they were in the right place.

"I've never noticed this building before," said Amber. She peeked through the keyhole. "Isn't yoga all that Indian stretching stuff?" She caught a glimpse of a poster. It was a man with his legs wrapped around his head. "I don't know if I could do that."

Jeremy shook his head. "It takes many years of practice."

Jeremy opened the door, and they crept inside. It was dark and empty except for a computer on a table in the middle of the room. The light from the screen made the table glow a pale green.

They walked over to the computer. The screen flickered with random images of India. They saw temples, rivers, elephants, cow-crowded streets, people's faces, lists, and facts.

When they reached for the mouse, the screen went blank. All that remained was the screensaver saying, "SWAT."

Suddenly, a voice came from the computer:

"Greetings, Jeremy and Amber. My name is Gosic. Your mission is to go to Mumbai and help Habbibi find his snake.

"In the drawer of this desk you will find two SWAT transporter wristbands.

"You must wear these wristbands at all times. They allow you to travel in the blink of an eye. Do not tell anyone that you are SWAT agents.

"There is also an envelope containing some rupees to spend when you get there. You must leave at once!

"Press **START MISSION** on the wristbands to begin.

"Good luck, SWAT."

Then the screen split into three separate images. One was a map of India, the second was a picture of Habbibi, and the third looked like fancy squiggles.

"That says '*aum,*' which means 'good luck' in Hindi," noted Jeremy.

"Hindi?" asked Amber.

"Yeah. That's the language most people in India speak," said Jeremy.

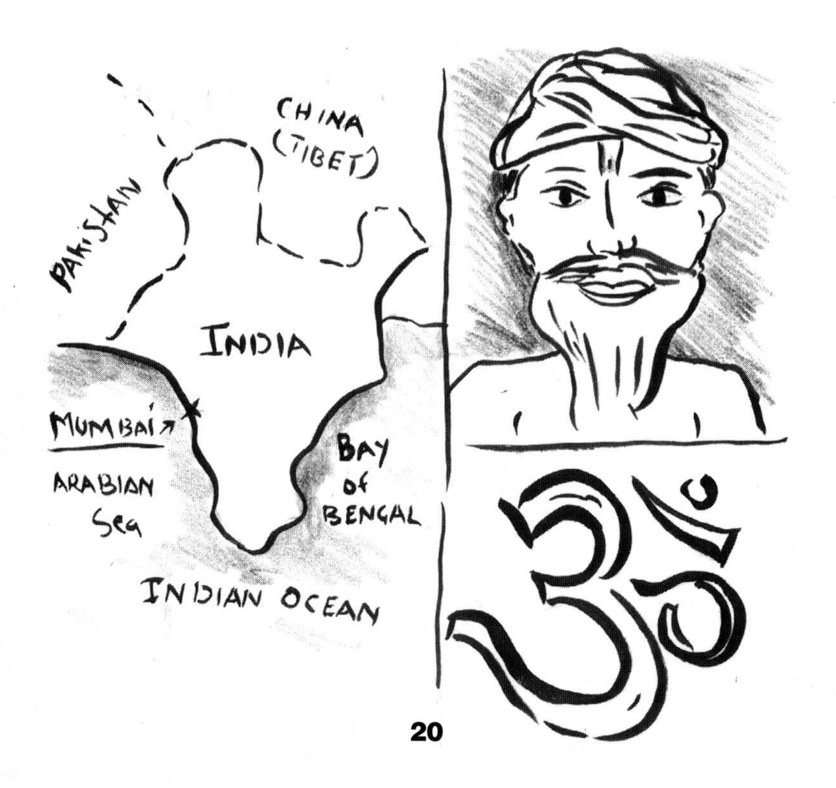

Amber noticed Jeremy writing everything down. "What are you doing?" she asked.

"I'm taking notes—like all good secret agents do."

The pair hunted in the drawer for the wristbands and the envelope.

"Ready, O.B.?" asked Amber. "Three. Two. One."

Click.

START MISSION.

CHAPTER 2

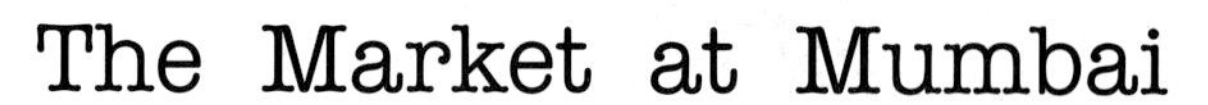

The Market at Mumbai

When they opened their eyes, they were in a busy marketplace. It was overflowing with strange and exotic goods. There were rows of powders in every shade you could imagine. Giant baskets were filled with spices with names like turmeric, coriander, cinnamon, cumin, and chili.

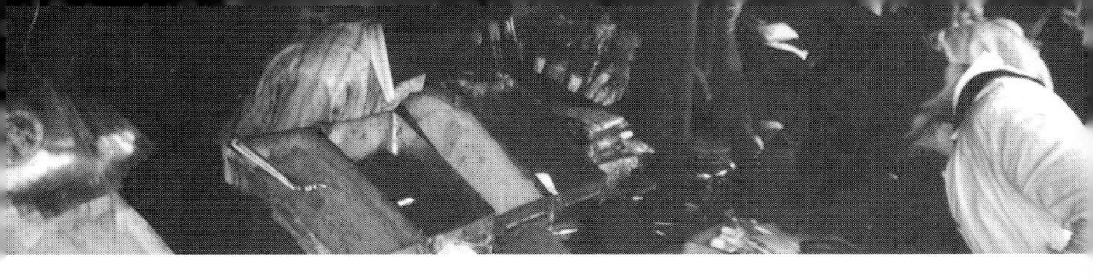

Ladies wrapped in colorful saris bartered with vendors, who were selling everything from rugs to jugs, bangles to bells. And all of the vendors yelled at the same time.

"Best silver in Mumbai!"

"Good price for jewelry!"

"Beautiful carpets—good price!"

Strange musical sounds filled the air. Amber could smell burning incense. It smelled of rose, sandalwood, and jasmine. But not for long!

Amber cupped her hand over her nose. "What on Earth is that stinky smell?"

"Cow," replied Jeremy.

Amber turned her head and came eye to eye with a big beast. "AHH! Go away!" she yelled.

"Careful," said Jeremy. "The cow is a sacred animal in India. You must treat it with respect."

There were many cows roaming freely in the marketplace.

Jeremy spotted Habbibi, the man they were supposed to help. He was sitting in a doorway next to a basket, holding a flute. As they walked over, Habbibi smiled.

"You have the whitest teeth, Habbibi," said Amber without thinking.

"Oh, thank you. Tell me, how did you know my name?" Habbibi asked.

Jeremy thought quickly and said, "A friend of ours said we would find you here."

"Ah!" said Habbibi. "You have come to see my famous snake charming act. But I'm afraid you are out of luck."

Amber and Jeremy didn't have the slightest idea what Habbibi was talking about.

"My snake was stolen from me a week ago, and I haven't yet found another, nor do I want to," said Habbibi.

"I don't understand," said Jeremy.

"You see," said Habbibi, "I loved that snake very much. It was such a good snake—a great performer. Very special."

Habbibi started to walk away.

"Where are you going, Habbibi?" asked Jeremy.

"To see a wise friend," answered Habbibi. "Both of you may join me if you wish."

CHAPTER 3
The Shaman

They left the chaotic market behind them and joined the city streets. The roads were alive and buzzing with carts, overloaded double-decker buses, and rickshaws. Horn-honking taxis, cars, mopeds, and wiggly bicycles overflowed onto the sidewalks. The sidewalks were full of people and cows.

Huge billboards lined the streets, promoting the latest Indian movies.

"Mumbai makes more movies than anywhere else in the world," announced Habbibi, as they came upon a long line of people waiting to get into the theater.

They saw business people and beggars. They walked by shops full of radios, silks, satin, and jewels. They passed doorway dentists and sellers of pots and pans.

Finally, they stopped at a door marked with a big eye. A man with long hair and a painted body answered the door.

"Wait here, please," said Habbibi before he disappeared inside.

"Who was that man?" asked Amber.

"He's probably a shaman," answered Jeremy.

"A what?" asked Amber.

"A shaman," Jeremy repeated. "He's like a medicine man—half priest, half doctor. People go to him and ask about life and the future and stuff."

Just as Jeremy said that, Habbibi bounded out the door.

"Oh, this is very good news," said Habbibi. "My wise friend says that you two will help me find my snake. You will recognize it by its eyes. Come, we must start looking right away."

Habbibi led the way through the maze of winding lanes to the train station. They passed people living in shacks made from whatever they could find—tin, sticks, cardboard, and cloth.

"This city is overcrowded," said Amber.

"Yes, it is," agreed Habbibi. "Mumbai has many problems because it is filled with so many people. There are not enough houses or jobs in the city, so many families are very poor and live in tents or shacks. Some families don't even have homes and must live on the streets."

"Habbibi, how will we recognize your snake by its eyes?" asked Amber.

"It has very special eyes, like no other snake. One is brown, and one is blue, just like the jewel, the sapphire." Habbibi stopped and waved to a rickshaw driver. "We will ride this to the train station to save time."

CHAPTER 4
Visiting Varanasi

At the station, Amber, Jeremy, and Habbibi bought tickets to the city of Varanasi in the north of India.

"Why Varanasi?" asked Amber.

"Because Varanasi is India's holiest city for Hindus. There is no better place to start our search!" cried Habbibi.

"We will go to the holy Ganges River," he continued, "and pray to the gods to return my snake."

They hurried up to the crowded platform to board the train. It was filled with animals, people, luggage, flies, and heat. It was hard to figure out who was getting on the train and who was getting off.

All Jeremy and Amber could see was a blur of saris, turbans, cows, children, chickens, baskets, and bags. People sat on top of the train as well as in it. The sun beat down, and flies zoomed all around.

Amber felt as if she was going to faint. "This heat and the crowds are too much for me to handle," she said.

A voice came over the station loudspeaker and said something very quickly in Hindi.

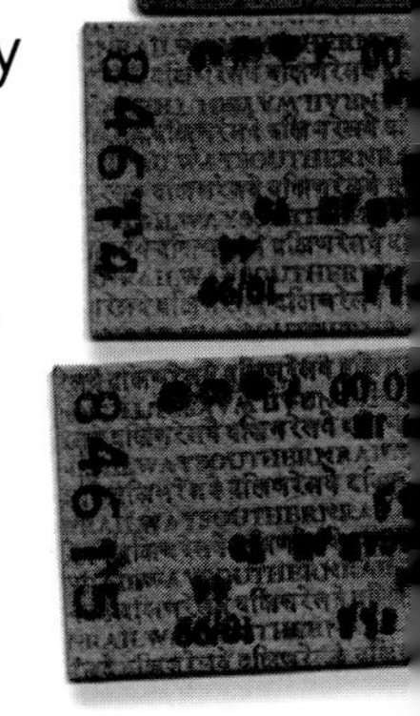

"Oh, this is very bad," said Habbibi. "The train has been delayed for a long time. We must find another way to get to Varanasi."

Jeremy and Amber huddled together and agreed to use their SWAT wristbands. If they held onto Habbibi, they could transport him, too.

"Habbibi," said Amber, "we know a much quicker way."

Jeremy grabbed Habbibi as he and Amber pressed the buttons on their wristbands.

"Varanasi, here we come!" said Jeremy. "Three. Two. One."

Click.

"Ahhhh! I'm all wet!" cried Amber.

"That's because you're standing in the Ganges River," laughed Jeremy. He had managed to land on the steps leading down to the river.

"How did you do that? It was amazing!" Habbibi sputtered.

Jeremy quickly changed the subject. “Come on, Habbibi. Let’s join Amber in the water.”

Habbibi was very excited. He had never been to the holy river before, and he stood looking out across it in amazement.

"What's so special about this river?" asked Amber, splashing in the muddy water.

"The Ganges is said to have special powers. Thousands of people come to the river every year to bathe in it," explained Jeremy.

Jeremy watched the holy men say prayers and pour water. Women on the steps held up small bunches of flowers. They offered them to the sun and then threw them into the water.

Farther downstream, people meditated. Men got their heads shaved. Others, in boats, performed ceremonies. Women collected water in jugs that they carried to shore on their heads.

The riverbank was a jumble of old buildings, spires, towers, and temples. As the trio walked past the temples, Habbibi told Amber and Jeremy about the Hindu gods.

"Krishna is the god of love, and this elephant-headed god is Ganesh, the god of luck and riches. This one, Kali, is the female goddess feared by all," Habbibi said.

"I'll be back in a flash!" said Amber, zooming down an alley. She returned a few moments later wearing a pink and orange sari and carrying a piece of cloth.

"This is for you," she said to Jeremy.

"Ah, a turban for Jeremy. Yes, that is good," said Habbibi. "Come, I will wrap it for you."

Habbibi tried to wrap the turban, but it kept falling off Jeremy's head. Jeremy couldn't keep still. He was too excited. He wanted to find the blue-eyed snake.

Amber and Jeremy asked people if they had seen a snake with one brown eye and one blue eye. An old holy man said he had seen one in a market a few days earlier. It was in the city of Agra, near the Taj Mahal.

Habbibi was very excited by the news.

"We must get there at once! Quickly! Quickly!" he yelled.

"Come on, Habbibi," said Amber. She grabbed his hand. "Let's go the quick way. Three. Two. One."

Click.

CHAPTER 5
The Taj Mahal

This time Amber made a perfect landing right in front of the Taj Mahal. Jeremy landed a few seconds later. Habbibi didn't question his new form of transportation. He simply said, "Very handy. One day I hope to be able to travel like this on my own."

India has many beautiful buildings, but none are more famous than the Taj Mahal. The white marble building glistened in the bright sun.

Amber gasped. "It's so beautiful!"

Habbibi proudly explained the story behind it. "It was built many centuries ago by an emperor named Shah Jahan. He was very rich, and he loved his wife deeply. When she died, he was heartbroken, so he built this in her memory. It took 20,000 workers 21 years to build."

"How romantic," sighed Amber.

They searched the temple, asking everyone they met if they had seen Habbibi's snake. Amber could see that Habbibi was quickly losing hope.

"Don't worry, Habbibi. I'm pretty good at finding things, and I'm lucky, too. Good things always happen to me," she said.

"In India, we call that good karma," said Habibbi, smiling. "Good karma is a reward for leading a good life. Now I am sure we will find my snake soon."

Finally, an old lady from one of the tourist buses gave them a clue.

"I was in the city of Jaisalmer yesterday," she said. "I noticed a man selling cheap camels in the market. He had a snake like the one you are describing. I remember because I thought it was odd that the snake had one blue eye. It reminded me of a blue gem. That blue-eyed snake was causing a lot of interest."

Amber and Jeremy grabbed Habbibi's hand, clicked their wristband buttons, and headed straight to Jaisalmer.

CHAPTER 6
Tales from Habbibi

Jaisalmer is a city in the Thar Desert. The travelers landed just outside the city walls as the sky was getting dark. Jeremy and Amber couldn't believe their eyes.

"Amazing!" they exclaimed.

The whole city was made of honey-colored sandstone and covered in carvings.

"Let's not waste any time," said Habbibi.

They roamed the winding streets and small alleys looking for Habbibi's snake. They found nothing. They searched the bazaar and asked the camel traders. No one seemed to remember anyone selling a snake with one bright blue eye.

Tired and disappointed, they decided to stop looking and have something to eat. They would continue the search in the morning. They ordered a variety of Indian dishes from a street vendor.

"What is this?" asked Amber after the first mouthful. "It's hot. It's spicy. I love it!"

"This is flat bread, this is bean soup, and the other food is curried vegetables," said Habbibi. "And it is OK to eat with your fingers. Just make sure to use your right hand, because eating with the left hand is considered bad manners here in India!"

Afterward, they set up camp in the desert outside Jaisalmer. Habbibi entertained Amber and Jeremy with stories of India's past.

He told them about Buddha, a holy man from long ago. Buddha sat under a bodhi tree for 49 days without saying a word or eating or drinking, and he experienced great things.

"That's how the religion of Buddhism started," said Jeremy.

Habibbi told them stories from long ago about men who traveled across the desert along the trade route. Jaisalmer was once a wealthy trading city.

From time to time, Amber would stare across the desert and see silhouettes of camels. Little cooking fires from other camps glinted, and turbans bobbed here and there in the dark.

"More stories, please!" begged Amber as soon as Habbibi took a breath.

He told them exciting stories of wealthy emperors, rajahs, and sultans who ruled India. Then he talked about a great Indian named Gandhi, who helped free India from British rule.

Habbibi talked long into the night, long past midnight. Slowly, the trio's eyelids got heavier, and the stories got slower. Finally, Amber, Jeremy, and Habbibi were sound asleep, huddled around the campfire.

CHAPTER 7
An Indian Wedding

"What is all that noise?" mumbled Amber, trying hard to wake up.

The sun was already high in the sky, and it was hot. A procession of people, singing and dancing, shook the ground. People were entering the city from all around, some on camel and some on foot.

"What's going on?" asked Amber.

"It looks like a wedding party," said Habbibi. "In India, people love to celebrate special days."

"That must be the bride." Jeremy pointed to a girl wrapped in a red sari. She was covered in jewelry and draped in gold tassles and flower necklaces.

Habbibi pointed to the young bride's hands and feet. They were painted with ornate designs.

"We call that custom *mehendi,*" said Habbibi. "Women decorate each other with dye made from the leaves of the henna plant. Let's follow the procession into the city. Maybe one of the guests will have seen my snake."

The crowd gathered in a beautiful courtyard inside the old city palace. The walls were covered with carvings, tiles, and paintings. Musicians gathered in the corner and played while dancers entertained the guests.

"This is unreal. Let's move closer to get a better view," said Jeremy.

One of the musicians played the drums, the other a flute. Another man strummed a strange-shaped guitar called a sitar. Beside him lay a canvas bag. Jeremy saw it move slightly, and he crept over to take a closer look. He moved the bag and opened the top just a fraction. A blue snake eye stared back at him.

Jeremy gasped. "It's a snake, and it has a bright blue eye!"

"My snake!" cried Habbibi. "My wonderful snake. You have been found!"

The band stopped playing. The dancers stopped dancing. All of the guests and the bride and groom stared in silence at the uninvited guests.

CHAPTER 8
The Snake Is Found

The groom frowned at Habbibi. "Who are you?" he asked.

Habbibi moved into the center of the courtyard and said, "I am Habbibi, the master snake charmer. I have traveled many miles in search of my snake. It was stolen from me in the market in Mumbai last week. I know it is mine because no other snake has one brown eye and one blue eye."

The groom walked over and peered into the canvas bag.

"It is true that the snake has one blue eye and one brown eye. Which one of you brought the snake?" he asked the group of musicians.

The man with the flute explained that it was his. He had bought the snake from a camel trader for a very good price.

"I tried to charm it to dance, but it would not move," said the man.

"I will prove this snake is mine," said Habbibi. "I will make it dance like you have never seen a snake dance before."

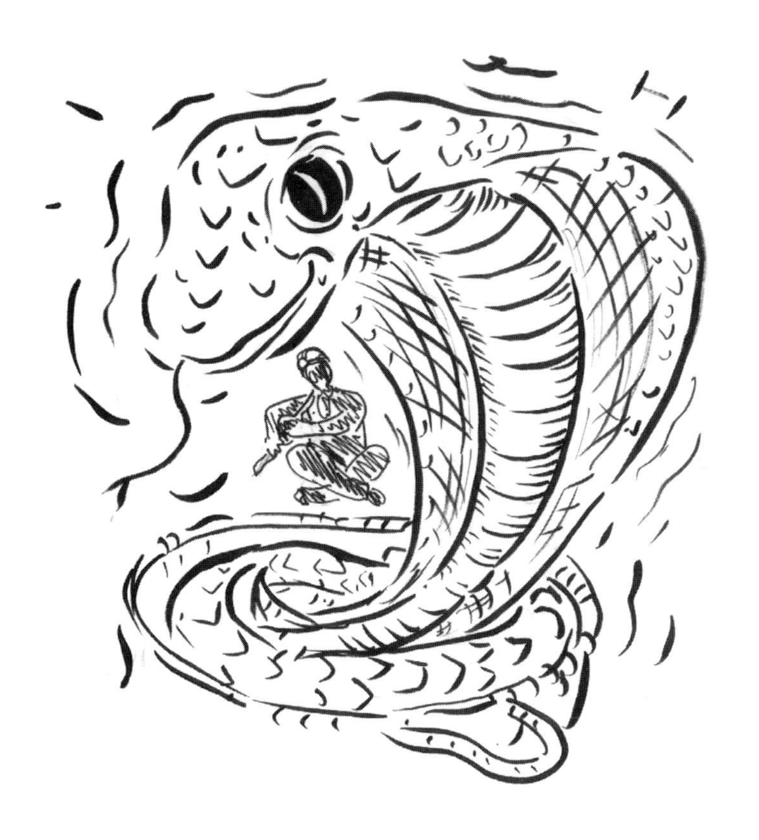

The musician handed Habbibi his flute, and Habbibi sat in front of the bag. As he began to play, Habbibi swayed from side to side. The snake raised its head and neck and followed Habbibi's every movement. It lifted its body as high out of the bag as it could. The crowd was mesmerized. Habbibi stopped playing, and the snake disappeared back into the bag.

"The snake is indeed yours," said the groom. He handed Habbibi the bag. "Come, I invite you and your friends to join in our wedding celebration."

He clapped his hands, and the music and dancing started again.

Jeremy and Amber felt their wristbands vibrate. It was a message from Gosic:

Congratulations, SWAT! Mission complete. Well done.

A red button appeared on their wristbands marked **MISSION RETURN**.

"It looks like we have to go, Jeremy," said Amber. "One found snake, one happy snake charmer."

"What did you just call me?" asked Jeremy.

"Ahh ...." Amber turned bright red. "It may just be the heat, but I don't think you're so odd after all. I mean, you make a pretty good SWAT agent. So, no more nicknames at school, OK? No more 'O.B.'"

"Really?" said Jeremy. "Well, you're not so bad yourself."

"Do you think Gosic would mind if we did a little sightseeing on the way home?" asked Amber.

Jeremy shook his head. "I've made a list of some of the things I'd really like to do. I'd like to ride an elephant and maybe see one of those Indian movies."

"Sounds great!" said Amber. "I just want to get some more of that yummy Indian curry, maybe another sari, and that henna dye, mehendi, and …."

"Three. Two. One," said Jeremy.

Click.

MISSION RETURN (with a few stops along the way).

GLOSSARY

barter—to trade by exchanging goods

beeline—the most direct route

chaotic—messy, noisy, busy, and dirty

henna—a red dye

Hindi—a popular language in India

incense—a coated stick that smells sweet when burned

karma—the belief that good things happen to good people and bad things happen to bad people

mehendi—body art made with henna

mesmerized—unable to look away

random—without order

rickshaws—small, two-wheeled carriages pulled by people

roaming—moving slowly from place to place

saris—long pieces of material worn by Indian women as dresses

shaman—a person who uses magic to heal people or to tell the future

silhouettes—outlines

sitar—a strange-shaped guitar

spices—tasty substances used for flavoring food

turban—a cloth wrapped around a person's head

TOOTH
मेंहदी